THE BOYFRIEND DILEMMA

"Hi, Katie, Christie, and Beth." Kaci Davis was brushing her blond hair and had seen them in the mirror.

"Got a big date with Jon, Christie?" Kaci asked.

"No, not really," Christie answered, trying to sound as casual as possible. "We're here together, but we're just friends."

Kaci's hand stopped in midstroke, and she looked at Christie's reflection. "Right!" Kaci nudged Colby Graham, an eighth-grader standing next to her, and they both laughed.

Christie could feel her face turning red. Not again, she thought.

Today had been full of the same things happening over and over. First she had had to explain about the mixup at the Super Quiz tryouts. Now she had to tell everyone that Jon and she were just friends. She held back an exasperated sigh and gave Kaci a forced smile. When would everyone finally get it?

THE FABULOUS FIVE

The Boyfriend Dilemma

Betsy Haynes

A BANTAM SKYLARK BOOK®

NEW YORK · TORONTO · LONDON · SYDNEY · AUCKLAND

THE BOYFRIEND DILEMMA
A Bantam Skylark Book / June 1989

*Skylark Books is a registered trademark of Bantam Books, a division
of Bantam Doubleday Dell Publishing Group, Inc. Registered in
U.S. Patent and Trademark Office and elsewhere.*

ISBN 0-553-15720-5

Published simultaneously in the United States and Canada

Bantam Books are published by Bantam Books, a division of Bantam Doubleday Dell Publishing Group, Inc. Its trademark, consisting of the words
"Bantam Books" and the portrayal of a rooster, is Registered in U.S. Patent
and Trademark Office and in other countries. Marca Registrada. Bantam
Books, 666 Fifth Avenue, New York, New York 10103.

PRINTED IN THE UNITED STATES OF AMERICA

CW   0 9 8 7 6 5 4 3 2 1

To Ken Slade
A dedicated educator

CHAPTER

1

"*A*sk me another question," Christie Winchell insisted to her four best friends. "I've just *got* to be ready for the Super Quiz team tryouts."

"How about this one?" said Katie. "The category is social studies. Who was the woman who led the fight for women's right to vote and had her head put on a silver dollar?"

"Her *head*!" shrieked Melanie. "Eeek! I'll bet that hurt."

Christie frowned at Melanie and then turned back to Katie. "You asked me that one yesterday," Christie protested. "Come on. Ask me something new."

"You'd know the answer to anything I could ask," said Melanie. "You're so much smarter than I am."

"Me, too," said Beth, running her fingers through her new haircut. It was short and almost spiky and fit her flamboyant personality better than her old hairstyle did. The short sides exposed the large fluorescent pink earrings she was wearing.

The Fabulous Five were gathered in the Winchells' family room and had been asking Christie all kinds of questions for almost an hour. Katie Shannon was sitting cross-legged on the floor. She was taking the questioning very seriously and had a notebook in her lap filled with pages of things she had thought up to ask Christie.

Melanie Edwards and Beth Barry were sprawled on the sofa eating potato chips and drinking sodas. Jana Morgan was looking through a history book, trying to find something to ask while Christie paced back and forth in front of them.

The Fabulous Five had been together almost forever. They had become fast friends when they first met in Mark Twain Elementary, and later they had started their club against Taffy Sinclair, the most stuck-up girl in elementary school. They were all in

Wakeman Junior High now, or Wacko Junior High, as most kids called it.

Christie had always been able to count on her best friends, and now they were helping her cram for the tryouts on Friday for the Wakeman Super Quiz team match against Trumbull Junior High. She had been picked to try out, along with Curtis Trowbridge, Whitney Larkin, and Melissa McConnell from the seventh grade, but only two students from each grade would be chosen to compete against Trumbull. Since questions about math, science, social studies, English, and current events would be asked, Christie wanted to be ready in every category.

"I think we've done enough for now," said Jana, closing her book. "You're answering nearly all of the questions and you don't want to overdo it. You need to peak during the tryouts."

"I guess you're right," agreed Christie. "But I'm afraid I'll overlook something."

"Yeah, and Melissa McConnell will jump for joy every time you miss one," said Melanie.

"So will Laura McCall," added Katie.

Christie knew her friends were right. Laura McCall and Melissa McConnell were two members of The Fantastic Foursome, the clique from another elementary school who had been feuding with The Fabulous Five from the instant the two groups had met on the first day of school.

"I don't have time to worry about them," said Christie. "The tryouts are only three days away, and I don't know *nearly* enough."

"Sure you do," said Jana reassuringly. "Besides, you can get Jon to help you, too. I'm sure he'd be glad to."

"Are you kidding?" asked Melanie. "Do you really think Jon's interested in doing homework when he comes to Christie's?" She winked at Christie knowingly.

"All you ever think about is boys," Katie said to Melanie. "Can't you get your mind off boys for a little while?"

Melanie laughed. "Sure. But why should I?"

"Actually, I kind of wish Jon wouldn't come over so often," said Christie softly.

"WHAT?" the others said in unison.

"Don't tell me the big romance is fading," said Beth, brushing potato chip crumbs from her lap into a napkin.

"It's not that I don't like Jon anymore. I do. I like him a lot. It's just that I've got so much going on in my life, and he always seems to be there. I guess I need a little space, now and then."

"Is he coming over tonight?" asked Jana.

"No. I don't think so. He's been using his camcorder a lot around school lately, and he's going to make one video out of all the ones he has taken. He was talking about going to the television studio where his mom and dad work to mix them. I'm glad he's going to the studio," Christie added. "I'd really like to be alone so I can concentrate on getting ready for the Super Quiz tryouts."

"Now that you mention it, Jon was at the football field yesterday," said Melanie. "He was taking pictures of the team and the cheerleaders during practice."

"I saw him with his camera in the cafeteria, too," added Jana.

"He's been taking all kinds of pictures," said Christie. "He's really interested in movie photography. For someone who used to feel as if he could never live up to his parents and their big television careers, he's not doing badly for himself right now."

"Maybe he'll videotape the Super Quiz and turn you into a game show star," said Melanie with a twinkle in her eyes.

Everyone laughed.

"Well, if we can help some more, let us know," said Katie, gathering her books and heading for the door.

"Thanks. I really appreciate everything you've done. You're great friends."

After the others had left, Christie gathered up the empty soda cans and put the chips away. In her room, she got out her schoolbooks and arranged them on her desk, putting the news magazines she had brought up from the family room on the floor beside the desk. They would help her get ready for current events questions. Finally, she grabbed a pad of paper, sharpened several pencils, and took her phone off the hook.

Now, she thought with satisfaction, I'll have two uninterrupted hours of good, hard concentration. That was all she needed, she was sure. She'd make the Super Quiz team or wilt her brain trying.

Christie opened her math book. Math was her best subject and it would be a good warmup. She moved the pad of paper to a better position and started to read. A few minutes later the faraway sound of the doorbell broke her concentration.

"Drat!" she said out loud to herself. Sighing, she got up to see who was at the door. Her mother was probably carrying a load of groceries and couldn't get her key out of her bag.

But when she opened the door, it wasn't her mother outside. Instead it was Jon Smith standing there with a big smile on his face.

CHAPTER

2

"Hi!" Jon's eyes lit up when he saw Christie, and she couldn't help smiling back at him. In spite of the fact that she hadn't wanted him to come over this afternoon, she was glad to see him.

Most of the kids at school thought of them as a couple. Christie guessed that was what they were, but right now she couldn't quite understand her own feelings. Sometimes she liked him more than a friend, but sometimes she didn't. She wanted so much to be independent, her own person, and she wanted the same thing for Jon, too. It was very confusing, and she had been thinking about it a lot lately.

"Hi. I thought you were at the television station working on your video."

"I was, but I started thinking about you and decided I'd come over," he said. "May I come in?"

Christie hesitated for a moment, remembering the books that were waiting for her on her desk. But how could she say no? She gave an inward sigh and stepped back. "Sure. Come on in." She led him to the kitchen and got sodas for them.

"I'm surprised you aren't studying," Jon said.

"Oh, I was, but it can wait a minute."

"How *is* the studying for the tryouts going?" Before she could answer, he added, "I think it's great that you were picked for the team."

"Thanks," Christie answered, adding a smile of appreciation. "Just because I was asked doesn't mean I'll be on the team against Trumbull, though. Curtis, Whitney, and Melissa are tough competition."

"They sure are," Jon agreed. "But I have confidence in you." Then he added, "Did I tell you that I'm going to do a video of The Dreadful Alternatives?"

"Oh, that's the new rock group that some of the kids at Wacko put together, isn't it?"

"Yes. And they're pretty good. I went to one of

their practices. They've got a great guitar player and the lead singer's not bad, either. They asked me to make a demonstration video to show to people who are considering hiring them.

"That reminds me." A note of excitement crept into his voice. "Do you want to see the video I just finished?" He pulled a black videotape from his jacket pocket. "It's something I'm doing that's kind of different. I'd like to get your opinion about it."

The thought of the books on her desk tugged at Christie again. She badly needed to study, but how could she refuse him when he was obviously excited? Christie was sure that he was extremely proud of the videotape, and he wanted her to be the first to see it. It made her feel good that he cared about her opinion.

"Sure," she said. "You go on into the family room and get it started. I'll get some chips."

By the time she had put chips into a bowl, Jon was sitting on the couch with the remote control in his hand. The television was turned on to a network station.

"Okay, what's it about?" she asked.

Jon smiled at her without answering and poked the remote control at the VCR that sat on top of the TV. The network picture vanished and the screen was blank for a moment.

Christie heard a low throbbing music, and a distant shot of the front of Wakeman Junior High came on the screen. Her first thought was that the quality of the picture was good and the music was a nice touch, but it was hard to understand why Jon was so excited about it.

Then the camera zoomed in on the school, and the school started turning over and over in time to the music. Suddenly the school disappeared and Wakeman kids were walking like Keystone Kops along the sidewalks. Then they abruptly changed directions and walked backward.

Just as quickly, they were gone, and the screen was filled with beautiful blurs of color. There were reds and yellows and greens and blues. The music turned dreamy and matched the soft feel of the picture. Christie sat forward, her eyes opened wide to absorb what she was seeing.

The camera focused and she saw the objects behind the colors. She let out a little squeal of delight. It was the gum tree in front of the school where kids stuck their gum before going in to class.

"I would never have believed that tree could look so beautiful," Christie said.

The scene changed again, and they were at the football field. The pictures and music raced along as the players ran and the ball flew first in one direction and then another. Then pictures of the cheerleaders were mixed in with the football players, switching back and forth, back and forth, between the cheerleaders and the players.

Before her mind could fully absorb what she was looking at, the camera was racing down a hall inside the school, and Christie caught her breath as she felt drawn into the madly speeding video. Suddenly the hall flipped over, and then they were in a classroom, and pictures of kids seated at their desks flashed across the screen.

As quickly as it had begun, the video was back at the front of the school and then zooming away to the original distant shot. The music and the actions both stopped, giving Christie an almost physical jolt.

Christie flopped back onto the couch and turned to Jon. His face had a worried look. At a loss for words, Christie just shook her head in amazement. But when she saw the cloud pass over Jon's eyes, she reached out and took his hand.

"Jon, what I meant was, the video is *fantastic*."

A smile brightened his face, and Christie could tell how much her opinion mattered to him.

CHAPTER

3

"How did the studying go yesterday after we left?" asked Jana. The Fabulous Five were seated at their favorite table in the cafeteria having lunch.

"Not great at all," answered Christie. "Jon came over after you left and wanted to show me the video he made. When he left, it was time for dinner, and after dinner I had my regular homework to do. I didn't work on the things I need to know for the Super Quiz team tryouts at all."

"That's too bad," sympathized Katie. "I thought Jon would be more considerate than that."

"I guess it really wasn't his fault. I didn't tell him how badly I needed to study."

13

"How was the video?" asked Beth.

"You wouldn't believe it," answered Christie, rolling her eyes. "It was the greatest. At first I thought it was going to be like a home movie. You know, boring. But he used the mixer equipment at the TV studio where his mom and dad work, and it was really good."

"Maybe I can get him to do a video of me when I become a famous actress," said Beth, striking a dramatic pose.

"Or he can videotape me in a great court scene, like one of the lawyers on *L.A. Law*," added Katie. She raised her eyebrows in mock seriousness and pounded on the lunchroom table with a banana as if it were a gavel.

Christie smiled at her friends' jokes. "I don't know. He may be too busy by then. He's going to do a demonstration video of that new rock group in school, The Dreadful Alternatives."

"Mandy McDermott told me she heard them practicing," said Katie. "I guess they're going to play at an assembly. She said they're really good."

"Wow! Do you know who their lead singer is?" asked Beth. "It's Kimm Taylor. I wouldn't want Keith hanging around her."

"Kimm Taylor? I don't know who she is," said Christie.

"You don't know her?" said Beth and Melanie in unison.

"She's that really pretty girl with the long black hair who went to Copper Beach Elementary," explained Beth. "She moved here last year from Hawaii. You might not have noticed her because she doesn't go out for any activities at school."

"*You* might not have noticed her, but all the boys have," said Melanie. "She's in my social studies class, and all the guys grabbed the desks around her."

"I think I know who you're talking about," injected Jana. "She's cute but pretty quiet. I'd keep an eye on her if I were you, Christie."

Christie felt a twinge of irritation at her friends. "Just because the band has a cute singer doesn't mean that Jon's going to fall all over her. But so what if he does, as long as he and I stay friends?"

"If you say so," said Katie.

Christie frowned at her, then lapsed into silence. Why couldn't anyone, even her best friends, understand that a boy and a girl could be good friends without romance? Besides, maybe it would be a good thing for Jon to get interested in another girl once she explained to him that she wasn't ready for romance just yet herself. It wouldn't really affect her own relationship with him, and she could get the space she needed so badly. The more she thought about the idea, the better it sounded.

"Do you want us to come over after school and help again?" asked Jana, pulling Christie back to reality. "We can even skip going to Bumpers if that would help."

"No, thanks," answered Christie. "I really need some time alone to concentrate. I've got to fill in the gaps in what I know, and the only way I can do that is by myself."

"Well, if you need us, just yell," said Katie. The others nodded their agreement.

Christie concentrated hard in each of her classes, temporarily forgetting about her dilemma with Jon. She didn't want to miss anything that might be asked in the tryouts.

Later, when she arrived at the media center for study period, it seemed as if everyone was getting ready for the Super Quiz tryouts. Curtis Trowbridge and Whitney Larkin were sitting by themselves with piles of books, and they were taking turns asking one another questions. I can't believe I can beat either one of them, Christie thought, trying not to panic. Curtis is really smart, and everybody knows that Whitney skipped a grade and is a genius.

At another table, Laura McCall, Tammy Lucero, and Funny Hawthorne were seated with

Melissa McConnell, questioning her. Now and then Funny would giggle out loud and Mrs. Karl would frown at her. Melissa wouldn't be easy to beat, either.

Christie looked at them through narrow eyes. Laura was the leader of The Fantastic Foursome. She lived alone with her father, who let her do just about anything she wanted, and she had great parties with no adults around. There were rumors that she made the others in her clique do things to stay friends with her.

Melissa McConnell was smart and very prissy and precise. She had run for seventh-grade class president against Christie, and every time Christie was involved in something, Melissa seemed to be on the opposite side. The Fabulous Five thought Laura was putting her up to it.

The other members of The Fantastic Foursome were Funny Hawthorne and Tammy Lucero. Funny was always laughing, and some people thought she was a bubblehead, but Jana thought she was nice. They were seventh-grade coeditors on the *Wigwam* yearbook staff.

Tammy Lucero was a gossip. She talked all the time and told everything she knew. The Fabulous Five suspected that she had started rumors about them a few times, but it was hard to know for sure.

Christie sighed. If she didn't get some time to study, Melissa, Curtis, and Whitney would all do better than she would at the tryouts. She found a table in a corner and spread her books out so people would see that she was busy. Finally, she thought, and opened her social studies book.

Just as she was reading the first sentence, something hit her in the back. She whirled around and saw Clarence Marshall and Joel Murphy standing behind her. Clarence was grinning at her, and his hair hung in his eyes, as usual.

"What are you doing, Christie?" Clarence asked. "Trying to get smarter?"

"She's already the smartest kid in the seventh grade," said Joel.

"Please leave me alone, you two," she said impatiently.

"Whoa! Let's not mess with old Christie," said Clarence. "Her mother's a principal, and she knows Mr. Bell. You mess with her and he'll send you to Teen Court."

"*Shhhh!*" Mrs. Karl pointed her finger at the boys and then at two empty seats.

Clarence and Joel headed for the chairs, snickering to each other.

"Hi. Can I sit here?" She hadn't heard Jon

come up on the other side of her and she jumped.

Christie fought back a frown. "Sure," she mumbled. But inside she was wondering how she'd ever get to study.

Jon sat down and opened a book. A few minutes later he looked over at Christie and poked her in the side. "Are you going to Bumpers after school?" he whispered.

"No. I'm going straight home so I can study," she answered.

"I'll walk you home."

"I'll really be in a hurry and would rather not," she answered.

"Oh." He went back to his reading.

A few minutes later Jon looked up again and asked, "Can I help?"

"No, thanks."

"What if I asked you some questions?" he insisted.

"No, Jon. Please. I need to study by myself." Christie instantly regretted the way she had said it. A hurt look passed over Jon's eyes.

"I'm sorry, Jon," she said softly. "I didn't mean to say it that way, but I do need to study by myself right now."

"No. I'm sorry," he said with a smile. "I didn't realize."

She gave him a smile of appreciation.

"Would Christie Winchell please report to the principal's office." The announcement came over the public address system.

Christie slammed her book shut in frustration. Mr. Bell, the principal, probably wanted her to be a messenger again. He was always asking her to take things to her mother. There was no way she'd be able to get in any more studying before tonight.

Everyone stared at Christie as she walked out the door, and Clarence Marshall and Joel Murphy covered their mouths and pointed their fingers at her.

"Oh, hi, Christie," said Mr. Bell's secretary, Miss Simone, as she approached his office. "Mr. Bell asked if I'd have you paged. He wondered if you would mind taking these papers to your mother." She handed a blue folder to Christie. "I don't know what we'd do without you, dear."

"No problem, Miss Simone," Christie responded. She took the folder and put it on her stack of books.

The last bell of the day was sounding as she hurried out of the office and ran directly into Tim Riggs. Her books spilled all over the floor.

"Hey! Don't you honk when you come into an

intersection?" he asked as he knelt to help her pick up her things.

"I thought the light was in my favor," she answered, laughing.

Christie had noticed Tim at the first Super Quiz meeting. He was tall, even for an eighth-grader, and his hair was dark and wavy.

"Are you ready for the tryouts?" he asked, flashing her a big smile.

"No way. Every time I try to study, someone interrupts me or something happens," she responded.

"You won't have any trouble making the team," Tim said as they walked toward the school entrance together.

"I wish I felt that confident," she answered. "I know how smart Curtis is, and Whitney skipped the sixth grade at Copper Beach Elementary. Melissa isn't a dummy, either."

"Look," he said, smiling at her. "I was on the seventh-grade team last year, and all you have to do is relax. The answers will come to you."

"If you say so," she said, laughing. Somehow Tim's easy-going manner made her feel a lot calmer.

They were chattering happily, and he was still carrying Christie's books, as they stepped out of the school doors. Out on the school grounds some kids were drifting toward the street while others stood talking in small groups. Christie let her smile freeze as she spotted Jon standing under the gum tree watching her and Tim walk out of the building. A strange look passed over Jon's face as their eyes met, and then he turned and walked away.

CHAPTER

4

Tim put the blue folder Christie had gotten at the office on top of the books he had just given back to her. "Don't study too hard," he said, flashing his great smile at her. She stood for a moment and watched as he walked away. He was nice—really nice.

A feeling of depression washed over Christie as she walked home by herself. Jon had looked so hurt when he saw Tim and her come out of school. If he had only waited to let her explain why she was with Tim.

But why should she have to explain? she thought angrily. She was her own person. She could talk to anyone she wanted. There was no reason she should ask Jon's permission to talk to another boy anymore than he should ask permission to talk to Kimm Taylor. They weren't really going steady. But still, she had never seen such a sad look in Jon's eyes.

When Christie got home, she grabbed a soda and a snack and was still in the kitchen when her mother came in.

"Hi, sweetheart," her mother said cheerfully. "How was your day?"

"Busy."

"Mine, too. Oh, by the way, did Mr. Bell give you something for me?"

"Miss Simone did. It's with my books."

"Good," said Mrs. Winchell. "It's the new budget forms. Would you believe that we're supposed to have our new budget finished already, and they haven't even given us the forms to do it on until now?"

Christie shook her head. Budgets sounded like one of the dullest things adults had to do.

"When I finish it, you can take it back to Mr. Bell to be passed along with all the others in our district."

Christie gave her mother the folder and went to her room to study. She tried hard, but the words didn't seem to want to stick in her brain the way they usually did. Her mind kept going back to Jon standing under the gum tree.

When she went to bed, Christie lay awake for a long time thinking about herself and Jon. They had been going together for almost two months, and she enjoyed being with him. She still cared for him, but she had so many other things to do—so many other interests that Jon didn't share. She was more concerned with grades and academic things while he loved to make videos. How could she do all those other things that *she* wanted to do if she spent all her time with Jon? When she finally drifted off to sleep, she was still feeling very confused.

"Did you know that Robin Williams stood on his head when he auditioned for Mork in that old TV show *Mork and Mindy*?" Beth asked The Fabulous Five as they stood at their favorite spot by the school fence the next morning.

"Why did he do that?" asked Melanie.

"So they'd notice him," responded Beth. "I'm thinking of doing something like that when I try out for the school play."

"Have you thought about going dressed as an Indian?" asked Jana. "It was lucky for you when Brain Damage was in town."

"It was lucky for *all* of us," said Christie. "I thought I'd die when Trevor Morgan asked us to come up onto the stage during their concert."

"No, I don't think an Indian would work," said Beth. "It has to fit the play. I wish I could just count on my brain like you can, Christie, for the Super Quiz team."

"That's easy for you to say," responded Christie. "But if I make it, it will be because Curtis, Whitney, and Melissa have had their brains freeze-dried."

"I heard that Trumbull has a *real* brain on their team," Melanie said. "His name is Rodney Cox and he's awfully arrogant. He never misses a question."

"He's one of the Trumbull guys we saw at the mall last week," said Katie. "You remember. They followed us and said those nasty things about Wacko girls being wacko. He was the tall one with curly red hair."

"I know the one you mean," said Jana. "He looked kind of like a nerd."

"That's him, all right," answered Katie.

"Well, they haven't met the Wacko team yet," said Beth. "Christie and the others will wipe him out. Especially since the match is going to be at Wakeman."

"We'll be pulling for you," added Jana. "The walk-through is this afternoon, isn't it? What's Mr. Neal going to do then?"

"He's going to show us how the contests are going to work. How to push the buzzer and all that kind of stuff," answered Christie. "I know you all will be pulling for me. I appreciate it, too."

"Did Jon come over again after school?" asked Beth.

"Well, no . . . I don't think Jon is very happy with me right now."

The others looked surprised.

"Did you have a fight?" asked Melanie.

"No. But Jon asked me if I was going to Bumpers, and I told him that I had to go home and study. He asked if he could walk me home, and I said I'd rather he didn't, I was in a hurry. Then I ran into Tim Riggs when I came out of Mr. Bell's office and dropped my books. You know, *really* ran into Tim— POW! Anyway, Tim picked them up for me and was still carrying them when we went out the front door."

"Well," said Beth. "What's wrong with that? Tim's cute."

"Jon was standing outside by the gum tree when Tim and I came out," Christie said, making a face.

"Oooh," said Jana. "Not good."

"That sounds like trouble," said Melanie. "What did he say?"

"Nothing. He just turned and walked away."

"That's the worst thing he could have done," said Beth.

"What are you going to do?" asked Jana. The school bell rang at that instant.

"Why should she do anything?" asked Katie as they headed for class. "She hasn't done anything wrong."

"I'll tell you more later," said Christie as they joined the crowd of kids moving into the building.

Christie rushed to her first class and opened her book for a few extra minutes of study.

"Okay, tell us *all*," Melanie said to Christie as The Fabulous Five put their lunch trays down at their usual table in the cafeteria. "You know how I love soap operas."

"Your whole life is a soap opera," said Katie. Melanie stuck her tongue out at her.

"There's really not much more to tell," said Christie. "I like Jon a lot. Besides you guys, he's my very best friend. We talk about everything."

"You talk about *everything*?" squealed Beth.

Christie's face turned red. "Well, not *everything*, silly. But almost everything. I feel as if he's my friend. I'd like to keep it that way, but I don't know how I can and not be romantic."

"You do have a problem," interjected Jana. "Especially since you have been dating. There aren't many boys that want to be *best* friends with girls and not get romantic and vice versa."

"I agree," said Katie. "If you like a guy well enough to be best friends, it's hard to imagine not dating."

"I didn't say I didn't want to go places with Jon and play tennis with him. I do. I'd just like to do it as friends."

The others looked at each other speculatively.

"Have you talked to Jon about it yet?" asked Jana.

"No, I haven't. I'm not sure how to tell him."

"Would right now be a good time to talk to him?" asked Beth.

"Why?" asked Christie, puzzled.

"Because there he is," said Beth, pointing.

Christie turned and saw him. He was carrying his tray to the return window. She gulped and then took a deep breath.

"Well . . . I guess I'd better do it," she said as she got up to follow him. "Wish me luck."

CHAPTER

5

"*J*on!" Christie called as she followed him out of the cafeteria. He spun around at the sound of her voice and stopped to wait for her.

Christie rushed to catch up with him. "Can we go outside and talk?"

He looked questioningly at her. "Sure."

When they reached the fence at the edge of the school grounds, Christie struggled to find the right words. "Jon, when you saw me with Tim yesterday, we were just talking. I accidentally bumped into him coming out of Mr. Bell's office and dropped my books. He picked them up and carried them to the door. That's all that happened. Really." She was suddenly frustrated with herself for being apologetic, but she couldn't stand to have Jon angry at her. Why were her emotions so mixed up? She wanted to tell him that she needed more space, but she didn't want him to be angry or hurt. How could she do both?

She hurried on while she still had the courage. "But I need to talk to you about something else." She hesitated, drawing in a deep breath. "You know I like you a lot, don't you?"

This time Jon smiled. "I guess I do."

"Well, I do. That's all there is to it. You should never doubt that." She put her arm through his. "Besides The Fabulous Five, you're my very best friend, and I want it to stay that way."

Christie took a deep breath and plunged on. "There's something I'd like to ask you, though. It's something I've been thinking about for a while."

"What's that?"

"This has nothing to do with any other boys. I don't like *any* other boy as well as you," she said quickly. "But I'd like for us to try being best friends for a while. Not boyfriend and girlfriend like we've been, but best friends."

As Jon turned to stare at her, Christie could tell he was hurt. She rushed to finish before she changed her mind.

"I feel like I need space right now. And it has

nothing to do with not liking you as much as ever. I just don't think I'm ready to go steady, and that's kind of what we've been doing. *Oh, darn!* I'm not saying it right." Christie bit her lower lip and frowned.

"I don't know how to say it so you'll understand." Tears came to her eyes. "I really don't want to hurt you."

As Christie turned away, she felt Jon's hand on her shoulder. He turned her around. "I thought we *were* good friends already," he said. "Maybe I was wrong."

"No, you weren't wrong about that. I just think we ought to date other people."

"Being best friends can't be all that bad," Jon said gently. "What do you want to do? I'm not sure I know how to be best friends with a girl."

Christie brushed away her tears. "We can do most of the things we've always done together."

"Okay," he said, raising his head high. "I'm not sure I totally understand, but I guess we can give it the old Wacko Junior High try." He looked at his watch. "I guess we'd better get to class."

"Oh, gosh! You're right," she said. "I've got to hurry. Everything is okay between us, isn't it? I'll see you later?"

"Sure," he answered. "I'll probably be in the auditorium before you're through with your walk-through meeting. I'm going to start taking videos of The Dreadful Alternatives."

Christie gave him the brightest smile she could manage, then hurried away to class.

By the time Christie got to the auditorium after school she was panting. Everyone else was already standing up on the stage with Mr. Neal. She rushed up the stairs and threw down her books just as Mr. Neal picked up his blue folder to take attendance.

Christie looked around at the other team members as he called their names. From the ninth grade there were Kyle Zimmerman, who was on the Teen Court with Katie, Pam Wolthoff, Holly Davis, and Andy Trudeau. Tim Riggs was standing with Brad Cochran, who was also an eighth-grader. Two other eighth-graders, Daphne Alexandrou, and Jenni Linn were talking near them. Curtis and Whitney were holding hands, and Melissa was sitting down, thumbing through a notebook. Talk about last-minute cramming, Christie thought.

"Okay, everybody, listen up," said Mr. Neal. He put down his folder and dodged a custodian who was sweeping the stage.

"This afternoon," he continued, "we're going to walk through all the steps that will be taken in the Super Quiz match so you will know what to expect

tomorrow morning at tryouts, and you can concentrate on answering the questions and not wondering
what to do next. We're lucky. The match with
Trumbull will be here at Wakeman, and you'll have
the home crowd behind you.

"First, I want you to take seats at the two long
tables set up here on stage. At the match, each table
will have two ninth-graders on the right, two eighth-
graders in the middle, and two seventh-graders on
the left. Today you can pretend that one team is
Wakeman and the other is Trumbull."

"We're Wakeman, they're Trumbull," yelled
Kyle and Andy as they raced to get seats behind one
of the tables.

"No way!" yelled Tim as he ran to the other
table.

"Okay! Okay!" shouted Mr. Neal. "Neither side
really has to be Trumbull. You'll just be two different teams."

Next, Mr. Neal explained that the ninth-graders
would be asked the questions in each category first.
As soon as one of them knew the answer, he or she
was supposed to slap the large button on the table at
that position. The light on the podium would flash,
and the buzzer would sound. Whoever hit the button first would get a chance to answer the question.
If it was answered correctly, that team got one point.

If the answer was wrong, the other team had a chance to answer the question on the rebound, and if they got it right, they got two points. Then the eighth-graders would do the same thing, followed by the seventh-graders.

As Mr. Neal was talking, Christie watched the musicians from The Dreadful Alternatives carrying their instruments onto the stage. There were two boys with guitars, a boy drummer, and a girl with a synthesizer. If the girl was Kimm Taylor, Christie thought, she's not that cute.

Just then Jon came up the stairs carrying his camcorder. He winked at Christie, and she almost melted with relief. Maybe he wasn't terribly angry with her after all.

Just as Christie was about to focus on what Mr. Neal was saying again, a thin girl with straight black hair that hung to her waist came onto the stage. She had big almond-shaped eyes and her skin looked as smooth as ivory. Christie did a double take. That must be Kimm Taylor, she thought.

Christie sneaked a glance at Jon. He was busy talking to the drummer and wasn't paying any attention to Kimm. What difference does it make anyway, Christie told herself firmly. Jon and I are just friends.

As the custodian started dusting the podium and

cleaning the tables, Jon's camcorder started making a *whrrring* sound. He was running around the stage taking pictures from different angles. Glancing back at Mr. Neal, Christie wondered how he could keep things straight with all the activity going on around him.

"After we've had a round of questions for each of the other categories," the teacher was saying, "we'll get to the current events category. Answers for the current events are worth five points each and can be answered by anyone, regardless of his or her grade. In the tryouts, however, we'll stick with answering by grade. During the Trumbull match, keep in mind that if you're wrong and the other team answers the question correctly on the rebound, it's worth ten points. A team can catch up really fast with current events.

"Does anyone have any questions?" Mr. Neal looked from student to student, and no one spoke. "Okay, study hard and lots of luck to you tomorrow."

"Are you feeling better now that we've had the walk-through?" Tim asked Christie as they all began to file out of the auditorium. She looked quickly to see if Jon was watching them. He was involved with the band and was looking the other way. Kimm was standing very close to Jon, and Christie couldn't help feeling a little twinge of jealousy.

"Much better," she said, giving Tim a bright smile. "All I have to do now is memorize a whole history book, a whole social studies book, a whole math book, and a whole science book."

"I hate to scare you, but the really tough part is the current events category. That's the one people really bomb out on. The only way to study for that is to read the whole encyclopedia and every current events magazine that comes out."

"Oh, great! What am I supposed to do about that?"

"Nothing." He chuckled. "Some kids got it, and some kids don't. You'll find out if you've got it when they ask you the questions."

"You're really encouraging," she said. "I thought I'd probably lie awake *half* the night worrying about the tryouts. Now I'll stay awake *all* night."

"Any little way I can help," he kidded.

When they reached the big double doors at the front of school, Christie stopped in her tracks.

"I've got to go," she said abruptly. "I'll see you tomorrow." Tim gave her a puzzled look and waved good-bye.

As Christie rushed away down the nearest corridor, her mind was racing. During the meeting she had noticed Tim looking at her several times. She liked Tim. He was fun to be with, and when she stood near him, she got goose bumps all over. But she liked Jon, too. Very much. Even if they had agreed to try being best friends, she didn't want to push it too fast by seeing someone else.

That evening, Christie spent most of her time cramming for the tryouts. She went through all of her books and made a zillion notes to remind her of the answers to possible questions. By the time she went to bed, she felt as if her head would burst from all the things she had forced into it. Every nook and cranny of my brain must be filled to overflowing, she thought.

Instead of lying awake the way she'd expected, she fell asleep almost as soon as her head hit the pillow. During the night she had a dream about Jon and Tim.

She was looking out a window, and the two of them were looking up at her.

"Go out with me," begged Jon, who was down on one knee. "I'll make you the star of one of my videos."

"Forget him. Go out with me," said Tim. "I'll help you study for the Super Quiz. I'll even help you do math problems."

"I'll make videos of you doing math problems," offered Jon, frowning at Tim.

Christie watched both boys carefully, hoping they wouldn't start fighting. She only wanted to be friends with Jon, and she had never thought about going out with Tim. In her dream she looked from one to the other in total confusion—not knowing how to answer either of them.

CHAPTER

6

"Okay, everyone," Mr. Neal called as the Super Quiz team regrouped in the auditorium the next morning. "Please take the seats you had yesterday."

After everyone was seated, he continued, "We almost had a big problem this morning. I couldn't find my folder with the tryout questions in it, but I talked to each of the contributing teachers and they gave me copies of the questions. You're probably surprised to find out that all teachers aren't perfect."

The boys made hooting noises, and the girls giggled.

"All right, I know you've been dying to do it, so get it out of your systems. *Hit those buzzers!*"

Hands flashed to slap the buttons that set off lights and the buzzers, filling the room with *baaap, baaap, baaap*. Christie laughed and fought off Curtis Trowbridge, who was trying to hit her buzzer, too.

"YOU CAN STOP NOW!" yelled Mr. Neal, and the *baaap, baaap* noises slowly quieted. Everyone was laughing and joking about who had beaten whom and who had made the most noise.

"Remember," Mr. Neal continued, "the top two scorers in each grade will represent Wakeman next Friday in the match against Trumbull.

"Now, I'm going to throw a switch up here at the podium, and from now on only the buzzer and the light connected to the button that is hit *first* will go off." Suddenly one buzzer sounded and a light blinked. Mr. Neal frowned jokingly at Brad Cochran.

"Okay, LET THE GAMES BEGIN!" Mr. Neal called out dramatically. The questioning started with the ninth-graders in the social studies category, and then Mr. Neal moved to the eighth-graders. When he began quizzing the seventh-graders, Melissa took an early lead in scoring.

As Christie had suspected, Curtis, Whitney, and Melissa were well prepared, and the competition among the seventh-graders was hot and heavy.

During the next round of history questions, Curtis passed Melissa, and Christie was next, with Whitney a close fourth.

The next category was science, which was Whitney's best subject, and she quickly pulled ahead of Christie. Christie began to worry that she might even come in last. She nervously tapped her fingers on the stack of books in front of her and noticed the edge of a blue folder sticking out from between the two books. Mom must have left this for me to bring back to Mr. Bell, mused Christie, pulling it out and laying it on top. I'll have to stop at his office after the tryouts.

Finally they came to the math category, and Christie was able to pull ahead of Melissa and Whitney. Now she was only a few points behind Curtis.

The questioning had been going on for nearly an hour, and the stage was very quiet except for Mr. Neal's voice as he asked the questions, the buzzer, and the voice of the answering student.

Christie saw that Tim was pulling ahead of the other eighth-graders. It looked as if he would make the team easily. He has looks *and* brains, thought Christie.

Then came the current events questions. Christie was amazed that she knew most of them, and she pulled into a tie with Curtis.

Mr. Neal held up an index card. "Okay, this is

the final question. Who is the number one ranked women's tennis player in the world?"

Christie slapped at the buzzer as quickly as she could and saw Curtis's hand hit his buzzer at the same time. Her number lit up.

"All right, Christie. You and Curtis are tied in points. If you give the right answer, you win first place. What is your answer?"

Christie couldn't believe the question was about tennis. She knew just about everything there was to know about tennis without even studying. She pulled herself up confidently and said as clearly as she could, "Steffi Graf."

"That's right," Mr. Neal said with a smile.

Christie sank back in her seat with a sigh of relief. She had made the team.

"Good going," said Curtis. "Congratulations."

She thanked him and looked across to the other table. Tim was smiling at her and Melissa was frowning. Melissa had come in third and wouldn't be on the team that played Trumbull. When Laura McCall found out that Christie would compete against Trumbull, and Melissa wouldn't, she'd probably be furious.

"Congratulations, everyone," said Mr. Neal. "You all did great. Those of you who didn't make the team for the Trumbull match will get another chance for our next competition. If any of the players who have been selected for the Trumbull match gets sick or for some reason can't compete, then one of you will take his or her place as an alternate. Lots of luck, everybody."

The kids rose from their seats and Christie picked up her books. As she tried to squeeze between the podium and Whitney, who was talking to Mr. Neal, her elbow was bumped and her books tumbled onto the floor. The blue folder fell open and a stack of index cards spilled out.

"Let me help," Curtis said. As he bent down to pick them up, Melissa pushed him aside.

"What are these?" she cried. "They're questions!" The room was totally silent as everyone looked at the cards and then at Christie.

Mr. Neal took the cards from Melissa and then picked up the blue folder from the floor. His face looked very grim. "Okay, everyone, the tryouts are over. Christie, could I talk to you in my office?"

The others left quietly. Christie saw Tim glance back at her. He gave her a weak smile and a thumbs-up.

CHAPTER

7

Christie sat in a chair in front of Mr. Neal's desk. Her mind raced as she tried to sort out what had happened. How had the cards gotten into the folder that Miss Simone had given her to deliver to her mother? Or was the folder really Mr. Neal's? It couldn't be. How could she have gotten it?

She felt like wilting in her seat as she faced Mr. Neal. She had never seen him look so stern.

"Tell me about how you got the note cards," he ordered.

"I don't know how I got them, Mr. Neal. Honest." She gave him a pleading look. "On Wednesday, Miss Simone asked me to bring home a blue folder from Mr. Bell for my mom. When I saw the folder with my books this morning, I thought my mother had given it back to me to return."

"You need to think very hard about how you got the note cards, Christie. It doesn't look good. I've known you for a long time and I've never known you to cheat, but you know how it's going to look to other people. When could you have gotten my folder?"

"I don't know. I just don't know," she said, making tight fists in her lap.

Mr. Neal sighed. "I hope you realize just how serious this is, Christie. I'm on your side, but I need help. If we can't find a way to prove you got the cards without knowing it, I'm going to have to take you off the match team with Trumbull. I don't want to suspend you from the Super Quiz team, but I can't promise it won't happen. It depends on how things go."

His words hit Christie like a bolt of lightning, and she sank back in her chair dumbfounded. Suspended from the Super Quiz team for cheating! That couldn't happen! She had worked so hard all her life to make good grades and to do the right thing. How could this be happening to her?

Her astonishment must have shown on her face. "I'm sorry, Christie," Mr. Neal added more gently.

"I don't want to do it, but right now it looks as though I won't have any other choice."

Christie's lower lip quivered and she fought back the tears that threatened to spill out. She clenched her fists so hard her fingers hurt.

"You think about it hard, Christie. If we're going to come up with anything, we have to do it by Wednesday so I'll know if I should tell Melissa whether or not she will be taking your place. Come and talk to me anytime you think of something that might solve it for us, Christie."

Christie whispered, "Okay," and got up and walked out of the room like a zombie.

What could she do? What could she say to her friends and everyone else? Mr. Neal would have to take her off the team for the match with Trumbull Junior High and maybe even suspend her from the team altogether. It would be the biggest embarrassment of her whole life. How could she face her friends and everyone else? What would she tell her parents? And Melissa McConnell, of all people, would take her place on the team. Laura McCall would have a field day over that.

As Christie walked down the hall, she felt like a convicted criminal. Tammy Lucero, the gossip of The Fantastic Foursome, was talking to Sara Sawyer and Heather Clark. They were looking at Christie, and she knew that Tammy was talking about her. Tammy and her Fantastic Foursome friends would tell everyone in school as fast as they could. Christie felt her face heat up and she turned and walked away.

When lunchtime came, she dreaded walking into the cafeteria by herself, so she stood outside waiting for one of The Fabulous Five. It was almost worse standing there by herself as Melinda Thaler and Alexis Duvall passed her and started whispering to each other. Christie knew they were talking about her. She was relieved when Tim stopped to talk. She could ignore everyone else.

"How's it going?" he asked. "Did you find where the cards came from?"

"No. But I didn't take them, *honest* I didn't. I don't know how I got them."

He looked sympathetic. "I believe you. What's Mr. Neal going to do?"

Christie's voice cracked when she replied, "He says that if we can't prove I didn't take them, he's going to have to take me off the team for the Trumbull match." And then she whispered, "He might even have to suspend me from the Super Quiz team. I've got until Wednesday to find out how it happened."

Tim frowned. "Can't you think of any way the folder could have gotten in with your books?"

"No. I just don't know."

"Did anyone touch your things at the tryouts?"

"I don't think so. I had them with me all the time. Why would someone do it, anyway?"

"To keep you off the team?" he asked.

Christie hadn't thought about that. Would Melissa McConnell have done it? When would she have had an opportunity to get Mr. Neal's folder and put it with Christie's things? She thought hard but couldn't think of when it might have happened.

"Tell you what," Tim said. "I'll ask some of the other kids on the team if they saw anything. Don't worry. We'll find out what happened." He squeezed her arm reassuringly.

"Thanks," said Christie. It was nice to have somebody on her side. Just then Jana and Katie came up.

"Hi!" they both chirped.

"Hi. I'll see you later," Tim said as he turned and left.

"How did the tryouts go?" asked Jana.

"Terrible," Christie answered. "You mean you haven't heard?" She was so glad to see her friends that the words tumbled out as she told them what happened.

"Gee," said Katie with a shocked look on her face, "how *could* you have gotten the cards?"

"I don't know," answered Christie. "That seems like all I've been saying, but *I just don't know.* Tim said he'd ask the other people on the team if they had any ideas."

"You don't think it was Melissa who put them there?" asked Jana.

"I don't know how it could have been," Christie answered. "But believe me, The Fantastic Foursome's not wasting any time telling people about what happened. I saw Tammy talking to Sara and Heather, and I know she was telling them about me. That's why I was waiting for one of you to come by. I didn't want to go into the cafeteria by myself."

"Don't worry," said Katie. "Just stick with us. We'll take care of Laura and her crowd if they try to make trouble."

Christie felt relieved that she was with two of her best friends. Jana, Katie, Melanie, and Beth would stick by her, no matter what. And Tim was trying to help. And there was Jon, too. Jon was one of her very best friends. He really cared about her and would definitely be on her side. There was no doubt about that. She could hardly wait to talk to him and see if he had any ideas to help her get this whole thing straightened out. He could surely come up with something. She felt relieved just thinking about it.

Jana and Katie each got on one side of her, and the three of them locked arms, straightened their backs, and held their heads high. Christie felt a swelling of pride as her two friends marched with her into the cafeteria.

She looked around the room defiantly, and the first thing she saw was Jon sitting next to Kimm. They were at a table in the corner sitting so close they touched, and they were laughing.

CHAPTER

8

*C*hristie's heart dropped into her shoes. What were Jon and Kimm doing together? She felt as if something had been stolen from her.

But no, she shouldn't feel that way, she reminded herself. She had told Jon she just wanted to be best friends, hadn't she? And she had even thought that his getting interested in Kimm or some other girl might help keep her own relationship with Jon from getting too serious. So why shouldn't he talk to Kimm?

But did he have to sit so close to her? He seemed to be having a lot of fun talking to her, too. Knowing that she and Jon were just best friends now didn't help that little feeling of jealousy that had crept into her at the sight of Jon and Kimm together. *He has every right to be with her*, Christie thought, pulling herself up to her full height.

She headed with Jana and Katie to their table without turning to look at Jon and Kimm again. Melanie and Beth were already sitting there.

"Christie," Melanie whispered as if she were a spy with a big secret. "What's this about your getting kicked off the Super Quiz team?"

Christie drew a deep breath and glared at the table where Tammy Lucero sat with the rest of The Fantastic Foursome. Laura McCall smiled back. Christie gave her an angry look.

"I have *not* been kicked off of the Super Quiz team," she insisted. "There's been a big mistake. Somehow I got Mr. Neal's folder with the questions for the tryouts mixed in with my books, and I dropped it and the cards with the questions spilled out. I don't know how I got the folder. *And that's THAT*," she added firmly.

"Sorry," said Melanie, drawing back. "I didn't mean to make you mad."

"*I'm* sorry," said Christie, putting her hand on Melanie's hand and smiling apologetically. "It's just that I think I've explained it a million times already.

"What am I going to do?" Christie implored as Melanie smiled back at her. "Tammy Lucero is telling everybody that I've been kicked off the team already. I know the rest of The Fantastic Foursome is doing the same thing, but Mr. Neal said I've got until Wednesday to find out what happened."

"Everybody knows you, Christie," said Beth. "They know you didn't have to cheat to win."

"You don't have *any* idea how it happened?" asked Jana.

"None at all."

"We could all spread the word that it's a mistake," said Melanie. "Like Beth said, everyone knows Christie wouldn't have to cheat to win."

"That's great," said Christie. "But if I don't find out what happened by Wednesday, Melissa McConnell will take my place in the match against Trumbull, and everyone will think I cheated, regardless."

"Let's put our heads together and figure it out," said Jana. "There's got to be a way. Why don't we all go to the auditorium after classes and go over the scene of the crime? If anyone can figure it out, we can."

"Right," said Katie. "The Fabulous Five can do anything."

"Oh, Christie, I heard you had a problem in the

tryouts." Laura McCall's voice suddenly interrupted their conversation.

None of them had seen her come up. She was smiling broadly, and Christie could tell she was over-joyed at Christie's predicament.

"It's none of your business, Laura McCall," said Beth.

"Just like the fact your boyfriend is sitting with Kimm Taylor is none of my business, Christie?" she said sweetly. "I guess you're right, only I hear you didn't do so well at the tryouts, and it doesn't look as if you're doing too well with Jon, either." She smiled her icky-sweet smile again.

"Some people win, some people lose," Laura said, flicking her braid over her shoulder. "Well, I don't suppose any of you Fabulous Five will be at the Trumbull match since *none of you* will be on the team. The Fantastic Foursome will all be there, of course, since one of our group *did* make the team."

"There's no proof that Christie took the folder with the questions," countered Jana. "In fact, we're sure we can prove she didn't have the folder. Some-one must have stuck it in with her books." Jana looked coldly at Melissa.

"Oh?" said Laura, raising one eyebrow. "I hear that someone saw Tim giving Christie a blue folder, just like the one Mr. Neal had the questions in, Wednesday after school."

For the second time that day Christie felt as if she had been hit with a brick. Everyone stared at her, even The Fabulous Five.

Christie dropped back down on the bench without even trying to explain that she had gotten that folder from Miss Simone. It hadn't been proven that she had taken the questions, and she had until Wednesday to prove that she hadn't, but that hardly mattered anymore. Laura McCall had just made it clear that Christie had already been found guilty.

CHAPTER

9

*A*fter classes had ended for the day, Christie trailed along after her friends to the auditorium. She couldn't help feeling gloomy about her chances of proving she was innocent, but her friends had insisted on going over what had happened.

"Laura McCall makes Joe Isuzu look honest," Katie said, giving her a sympathetic look. Christie smiled at her friend gratefully.

"Okay, Christie. Tell us exactly what happened during the tryouts," ordered Jana.

"Well, we came in, and Mr. Neal told us to sit where we had been sitting the day before."

"Where *was* everyone sitting?" asked Melanie. "Show us."

"Kyle Zimmerman and Holly Davis were sitting on one end, Daphne Alexandrou and Brad Cochran were in the middle. I was next to Brad and Curtis was next to me."

"Where was Melissa?" asked Katie.

"Over there, at the other table," answered Christie, pointing.

"Where did you put your books?" asked Jana.

"I put them right in front of me on the table where I was sitting."

"Did you put them down someplace else before you sat down?" asked Beth.

Christie bit her lower lip and thought a moment. "No . . . I had them in my arms until I sat down."

Her four friends' eyebrows wrinkled into frowns almost in unison.

Katie walked over to the podium. "You didn't talk to Mr. Neal and put the books down over here, did you?"

Christie shook her head. "I *didn't* put the books down, except at the table where I was sitting. And *no one* came near them. That's why I can't understand how the folder got in with my books."

"Curtis or Brad?" asked Jana. "They were sitting next to you. Could either one of them have done it?"

Everyone looked at her.

"Why would they?" asked Katie. "There has to be a motive."

"Speaking of motives," said Beth, "Laura said she heard that *Tim* gave you a blue folder. You have to admit that he's been hanging around you a lot ever since the tryouts started."

"Right!" said Jana excitedly. "And he's a real brain so he's sure to make the team."

"Are you guys thinking what I'm thinking?" asked Melanie, nodding to the others and opening her eyes dramatically. "He wanted to make sure Christie made the team, too, so he gave her the questions without her knowing it."

"He wouldn't do that," Christie insisted. "Besides, I know the folder he handed me was the one Miss Simone gave me to take home to my mother. There has to be something else."

"But what?" asked Jana.

The Fabulous Five stared at each other in gloomy silence. "I don't know what else to tell you," said Christie quietly. "That's all that happened." She felt the tears beginning to well up in her eyes again.

Jana came over to her and hugged her. "Keep thinking, Christie. We all believe you didn't do it, and there has to be an explanation."

"That's right," said Katie, wrapping her arms around both Christie and Jana. As Beth and Melanie joined them, Beth raised her hand for a high five and shouted, "One for all, and all for one!" The others slapped it, but Christie could tell they weren't enthusiastic. They knew, just as she did, that her chances of finding out how she had gotten the Super Quiz questions before the Wednesday deadline were pretty slim.

Christie braced herself as The Fabulous Five entered Bumpers. The room was filled, as usual, with the after-school crowd, and the old Wurlitzer jukebox was blaring loudly. Mr. Matson, the owner, was working the cash register as kids lined up with sodas, dishes of french fries, and hamburgers.

"All the booths are filled," said Christie.

"Why don't we stand by the jukebox? That way all the boys can admire us," suggested Melanie.

"Yeah," agreed Beth. "And we can talk to them when they come up to play songs."

"Who wants a cola?" asked Katie cheerfully. "I'll go get them if somebody will help."

"I do and I'll help," said Melanie. "I see Scott in line and I want to talk to him." Christie, Jana, and Beth gave them their orders.

"There's Randy," said Jana. "I'll be right back."

Then she added, looking at Christie, "I'll be watching in case you need help."

Christie surveyed the crowd, telling herself that she was *not* looking for Jon but knowing deep down that she dreaded the possibility of seeing him with Kimm again.

Dekeisha Adams and Mandy McDermott were sitting with Bill Soliday and Tony Sanchez. Dekeisha waved when she saw Christie and Beth. Laura McCall and her friends were sitting together, and when Christie noticed them, they started whispering to each other and pointing in her direction. Christie had the feeling it was all for her benefit.

"Hi," said Shelly Bramlett as she came up to put money in the Wurlitzer.

Christie and Beth said "Hi" back.

"Did I see Jon sitting with Kimm Taylor in the cafeteria today?" Shelly asked Christie as she punched the buttons. "You and Jon haven't had a fight, have you?"

Christie tried not to show any reaction to Shelly's question. "Oh, no. Jon and I aren't going steady. We're just good friends."

Shelly looked at Christie. "Hey, Christie. I think you're prettier than Kimm Taylor any day. You don't have to worry about her."

"I'm not worried about Kimm Taylor," responded Christie. "Jon can talk to her all he wants."

"Well, if he were my boyfriend, I wouldn't let someone take him away without a fight," said Shelly. "See you later."

Christie looked at Beth. Beth shrugged noncommittally. Why can't people understand about Jon and me? Christie wondered. But still, Shelly's words left her feeling depressed.

Looking around again, she saw Jon sitting with Keith Masterson and Randy Kirwan at the booth where Jana had gone to talk to Randy. Jon gave Christie a big smile when he saw her.

"Here are your sodas," said Katie, coming up from behind them. "Where's Jana?"

"Over there, talking to Randy," answered Beth.

"I'm glad I got in line. Scott just asked me if I'd go to the movies with him tonight," said Melanie. "Is anyone else going?"

"I'm going with Tony," answered Katie. "We're going to double with Jana and Randy. Randy's dad is dropping us off."

"Keith and I are going, too," said Beth. "Why don't we all meet in front and sit together."

"That sounds great," responded Katie. "What about you, Christie? Are you and Jon going?"

"We haven't talked about it," answered Christie. "I don't know what he's doing."

"Are you two still just best friends?" asked Katie.

Oh, no, thought Christie, glancing in Jon's direction. Not more questions about us.

"Nothing has changed," she answered, trying not to show her frustration at the question.

Going to the movies with The Fabulous Five and their boyfriends was always fun, but she didn't really have a boyfriend of her own now, and Jon might not want to go with her. He might want a *real* date.

"Look out, here comes Laura and her friends," whispered Beth. Laura, Melissa, Tammy, and Funny had gotten up from their booth and were headed toward The Fabulous Five.

"Have you found the *mystery* person who *supposedly* put the answer cards in your folder?" asked Laura. She had the end of her long braid in her hand and one eyebrow was raised arrogantly.

"It's just a matter of time until we do," Christie said with more confidence than she really felt.

"There are only a few people in Wakeman who would do such a dirty trick," said Beth, stepping forward. Christie knew Beth wanted to protect her from Laura's insults and appreciated her friend's efforts.

"Well, you don't have a lot of time left," interjected Melissa.

"I've got until Wednesday," responded Christie.

"Maybe not," said Tammy with a sneaky grin.

Christie looked at her questioningly. "What do you mean? Mr. Neal said I had until then."

"Well," piped up Melissa, "*we* don't think it's fair for me to have to wait that long to know if I'm going to be on the team, and I'm going to tell Mr. Neal that. After all, I need to know whether or not I should study, don't I? Wednesday is too late to find out. *We* think he'll change the day to Monday." The Fantastic Foursome smiled in unison, although Funny Hawthorne seemed uncomfortable.

"Studying won't do you any good," said Melanie. "You've got *too* much to learn." She and Melissa gave each other angry looks.

"*We'll see*," said Laura. She turned and headed for the door with Melissa, Tammy, and Funny following her.

"I'm glad they're gone," said Katie. "Do you really think Mr. Neal would change the date on you, Christie?"

"I don't know. I bet they ask him to, though."

"Hey, Christie. Things are looking up," said Melanie, nudging her. "Here comes Jon. Maybe he's going to ask you to the movies."

Christie turned and saw Jon headed toward them. Was Melanie right? Was he going to ask her for a date? Or was it something else? Maybe he liked Kimm so much now that he wanted to break off everything, even his friendship with Christie. Maybe she had been wrong to think that a boy and a girl could just be best friends. She cringed at the thought of losing him completely, especially now that she needed his help and his friendship so badly. She looked questioningly at him as he approached, but she couldn't tell anything from the expression on his face.

CHAPTER

10

"I'm out of here," said Beth as Jon came toward them. "I want to talk to Keith anyway, and you and Jon don't need us hanging around." She puckered her lips and made a kissing sound at Christie.

"Me, too," said Melanie. "I don't want to be near if you two decide you've had enough of this boy-girl friendship stuff. I don't know if I could survive the explosion of your first making-up kiss."

"I'm going to sit with Jana," said Katie. "See you all at the movies tonight."

"Boy, I sure made them scatter," said Jon as he came up beside Christie. "Isn't my deodorant working?"

"They had people they wanted to talk to," answered Christie. "It wasn't you."

"When you're ready, can I walk you home?" he asked. "Can best friends do that?"

Christie almost crumpled with relief. Kimm or no Kimm, he did still care about her. "Of course. Best friends do things like that all the time," she said. She wanted him to really believe that she meant he was her best friend outside of The Fabulous Five. "I'm ready to leave anytime you are." Christie noticed people watching them as they walked out of Bumpers.

"What's this rumor going around about your having trouble with the Super Quiz team?" asked Jon.

Christie patiently explained it for what she thought must be the zillionth time. She had never been so tired of talking about one thing in her life, but she wanted Jon to understand how serious things were and just how much she needed his help.

Jon frowned. "Everybody knows you wouldn't do a thing like that, of course."

"Melissa McConnell and her friends are telling everyone I did. Also, she's going to ask Mr. Neal to make a decision about whether or not I'm on the team by Monday instead of Wednesday. She's the first alternate and says she needs the extra time to study for the match with Trumbull."

"So even if they aren't responsible for your problem, they're taking advantage of it," he said.

Christie nodded. "If you think of anything . . . anything at all . . ." Her voice trailed off. She wanted to tell him how desperately she needed his help and ask him to call her and come over and spend all the time with her that he could while they found a way to work her problem out. But now that he was spending time with Kimm, would he think she was simply jealous? Or would he want to tell Kimm everything and ask for her help, too? Christie shuddered at that thought. She certainly didn't want Kimm poking around in her private business, but if she was Jon's girlfriend then maybe . . .

Jon must have read worry in her expression because he put his arm through hers, and they were quiet for a while as they walked along the street leading to her house.

It was Jon who finally broke the silence. "Don't worry. You didn't do anything wrong, and we'll prove it." Before she could respond, he added, "Are you doing anything tonight?"

She looked at him. His eyes were full of expectation.

"No," she said softly.

"I was wondering if a best friend, who just happens to be a boy, could ask a best friend, who just happens to be a girl, to go to a movie?"

Christie hesitated. Questions swirled in her mind. What about Kimm? And was he really asking her as a best friend? Or did he want to date her? Would it complicate things if she said yes? What would happen when he took her home? Would he want to kiss her? Or would they be proving that they could be best friends and go places together?

"I mean it," he said. "I started thinking about what you said, and I think maybe you were right. A guy and a girl should be able to be best friends like two guys or two girls. It's just that we'd be doing something new, and the idea takes a little getting used to."

"Had you thought about asking Kimm Taylor to go with you?" Christie asked.

Jon got a surprised look on his face. "To be honest with you, I did think about asking Kimm, but I decided I wanted to ask you instead."

Christie was quiet for a moment, thinking. "Why?" she asked.

"I know you're having a hard time now, and people don't seem to want to believe that a guy and a girl can be best friends. I thought we ought to show them that you and I can do it."

"Are you sure you wouldn't rather go with Kimm?"

"No. I'd rather go with my best friend," he replied.

Christie squeezed his arm. "I'd love to go to the movie with you tonight. We'll show everybody. We'll both pay our own way, right?"

"Right," Jon said with a laugh, and Christie felt light-headed with relief.

The line at the movie theater was long, and Christie pulled the money for her ticket out of her pocket as she and Jon got on at the end. Jana and Katie were already on line with Randy and Tony.

"Beth and Melanie are inside!" called Jana. "They're going to save a row of seats for us!"

Christie nodded.

"Hi, Christie! Hi, Jon!" Dekeisha Adams yelled as she joined Dan Bankston, who had just bought tickets for them.

Christie waved back and said to Jon, "Dekeisha and Dan make a nice couple, don't they?"

He looked at her with a half-smile on his face and

nodded agreement. *Ooops!* Christie thought. Why did I automatically assume they're a couple? Why can't they just be best friends going to a movie, like Jon and I? She was expecting Jon to think that way, and yet even she didn't all the time.

She didn't know what to say to Jon after that, and the silence hung between them like a thick curtain. Christie wondered if he was thinking about her comment.

Why did girl-boy relationships always have to come down to dating or hardly knowing each other? Jon and she had talked about a lot of things . . . just like best friends. She sneaked a glance at him. I wonder if he has told anyone some of the things I've told him? Like what I said about Melanie and Beth? He *wouldn't* do that, she assured herself. But she looked at him and wondered in spite of herself.

She had told him how boy crazy she thought Melanie was. But the rest of The Fabulous Five thought that, too. Katie was always asking Melanie if she ever thought of anything else but boys.

And Beth was so theatrical. Christie had confided in Jon that she thought Beth was a little bit of a show-off and that she said some pretty wild things at times. It was the kind of thing she would have said to any of The Fabulous Five. But she had told Jon, not one of them. And as far as Christie knew, Katie didn't tell *anyone* outside of The Fabulous Five that she thought Melanie was boy crazy. If Jon got mad at her, would he tell someone else what she had said about Melanie and Beth? As much as she didn't think he would, the thought made her uncomfortable, as if she were a traitor.

Inside the theater it was a madhouse. Kids were moving in and out of the rows of seats to talk with friends, and every once in a while an empty popcorn box would go whizzing through the air.

Christie held on tightly to her popcorn as Jon led her down the aisle, zigzagging through the crowd. Finally they reached the row that Beth and Melanie had saved for The Fabulous Five and their dates. Jana and Randy moved in so Jon and Christie could have the seats nearest the aisle.

Elizabeth Harvey, who had been elected secretary of the seventh-grade class when Christie had run for president, saw her and stopped in the aisle to talk.

"Hi, Christie. Hi, everybody." She waved to the others. "Is it true that you might not be on the Super Quiz team, Christie?"

Christie took a deep breath and said, "I don't

know yet. There's been a mixup, but I think everything will be all right."

"I wouldn't believe everything you hear," Jon added. "There's just been a mistake. *Everyone* knows Christie didn't do anything wrong."

"I hope so," said Elizabeth. "But you and I are prejudiced because I like Christie and you're her boyfriend. Sometimes the right thing doesn't always happen, you know."

"You're not making our day," Jon grumbled.

"Oh, I'm sorry. I'm sure everything will turn out okay. Have a good time, you two," Elizabeth said with a knowing smile.

Christie cringed. Why did Elizabeth have to make those remarks about Jon's being Christie's boyfriend? Couldn't *anyone* realize that just because she and Jon were at the movie together didn't mean they were going steady or that they were going to have a big love scene later. Was Jon embarrassed at what Elizabeth had said? Christie couldn't tell.

"I've got to go to the ladies' room," said Beth. "Does anyone want to go with me?"

"I'll go with you," said Christie.

"Me, too," said Katie.

There was a long line in the ladies' room, and they had to wait their turn. Christie dug in her purse for a tissue.

"Hi, Katie, Christie, and Beth." Kaci Davis was brushing her blond hair and had seen them in the mirror. Kaci was a pretty ninth-grader who was on the Teen Court with Katie.

"Got a big date with Jon, Christie?" Kaci asked.

"No, not really," Christie answered, trying to sound as casual as possible. "We're here together, but we're just friends."

Kaci's hand stopped in midstroke, and she looked at Christie's reflection. "Right! Just like Katie's only friends with Tony Calcaterra." Kaci nudged Colby Graham, an eighth-grader standing next to her, and they both laughed.

Christie could feel her face turning red. Not again, she thought.

Today had been full of the same things happening over and over. First, she had had to explain about the mixup at the tryouts. Now she had to tell everyone that Jon and she were just friends. She held back an exasperated sigh and gave Kaci a forced smile. When would everyone finally get it?

To make things worse, the movie wasn't as great as Christie had thought it would be. Maybe it was because she had ducked down to keep from being seen every time someone she knew came by their row. It didn't work, though. If kids didn't see her at first, they saw one of the other Fabulous Five and stopped. Then they saw her, and inevitably there would be a comment about Jon and her going together.

She did find a quarter and a dime on the floor, however, which was the good part. The bad part was that she bumped her head against the seat in front of her and a glob of gum stuck to her forehead. She was *very* glad when the credits came on the screen and the movie was over.

Jon didn't take her hand the way he usually did as they made their way out of the theater. She decided it was probably for the best even though it made her a little sad. Why couldn't people understand that boys and girls could like each other and not always have to have romantic relationships? This just might be the most miserable day in my whole life, Christie thought. First, I'm accused of cheating at the tryouts, and now people won't let Jon and me have a normal friendship.

Jon didn't say anything as the two of them stood at the curb away from everyone else waiting for his dad to pick them up. Was Jon upset about all the questioning? He hadn't even suggested that they go to Bumpers with the rest of the crowd. Would he want to be seen with her after this evening? She looked at his handsome profile. Most girls would love to have Jon as a boyfriend. *But I'm not ready to go steady*, she thought stubbornly. She glanced in the direction Jon was staring. Kimm Taylor was looking at them and smiling. Or was she just smiling at Jon?

CHAPTER

11

*E*xcept for Mr. Smith's attempts to make conversation, the ride home from the movie was made in silence. For the first time that she could remember, Christie felt ill at ease sitting next to Jon. The evening, which she thought would prove that they could be best friends, had turned out to be a disaster.

When they reached Christie's house, Jon had walked her to the door, and they stood there, neither one of them seeming to know what to do or say next. At one moment she thought he was going to kiss her, and she almost wanted him to. She wasn't sure. She liked him so much, but she just didn't feel as romantic about him as she had before.

Instead of kissing her, he looked at her, said good-bye, and walked back to the car. She stood on the porch watching as the taillights of his car disappeared around the corner of the block.

Later, Christie tossed and turned in bed. Everything in her life was a mess. Jon had been awfully quiet when he dropped her off. Was he disturbed by the way the evening had gone, or was he mad at her? People never stopped asking questions about their going together, and everyone except her best friends thought she had cheated on the Super Quiz tryouts. Even Mr. Neal, whom she had known ever since he was her fifth-grade teacher at Mark Twain Elementary, probably thought she was a cheat.

How had she gotten Mr. Neal's folder with the questions? If she could just figure that out, at least she would solve one of her problems. She went over her movements of the last few days in detail one more time.

She had gotten a blue folder from Miss Simone on Wednesday. Then she ran into Tim outside the office and dropped her books. Tim had helped her pick them up and had given them and the folder back to her outside on the school grounds. She had thought that was the folder with her books on Friday, but it wasn't. She had checked with her mother, and Mrs. Winchell had assured her that she still had the folder Mr. Bell had sent her containing forms for the budget.

Thursday had been normal. She had gone to all of her classes. She had kept her things, except for what she needed, with her or in her locker.

Then there was the walk-through meeting for the tryouts. But she couldn't remember anything unusual happening then. The Dreadful Alternatives had come on stage, but she couldn't recall their getting near the Super Quiz team. Oh, yes, Jon had come out with his camcorder and started taking pictures. There was nothing else. She had gone straight home to study on Thursday evening. So she couldn't have picked the folder up at Bumpers. Her mind whirled with confusion. There *had* to be an answer. There was an answer to *everything*. She could figure out any math problem. Why couldn't she figure this one out?

It was well into the night before Christie went to sleep. And then she tossed and turned and had dreams about being in jail and Laura McCall and her Fantastic Foursome friends standing outside her cell laughing and pointing at her. Jon stood by himself off to the side, watching but not saying anything. She heard hammering outside, and when she looked outside her cell window, she saw The Fantastic Four-some out there. They were pounding nails into a platform with a trapdoor in the bottom. A rope hung from a crossarm, and Kimm Taylor was tack-ing a sign up that read:

BIG CELEBRATION MONDAY
THE HANGING OF CHRISTIE WINCHELL

The next morning was Saturday, and Christie slept later than usual. When she looked at her face in the mirror, she couldn't believe the red rings around her eyes. When she went downstairs, she discovered that her mother and father were already out. Chris-tie was just finishing her toast when the phone rang.

"Christie?" It was Jana. "Are you going to the Milford football game today? It's an important game. If we win we'll be four and oh and in first place."

"I don't know. I don't think I could stand to have people ask me anymore about the Super Quiz team. I am really *sick* and *tired* of talking and thinking about it."

"Have you come up with any new ideas?" asked Jana softly.

"No. None at all," Christie said tiredly. "I've

thought and thought until I can't think about it any-more. I was awake all night thinking about it." She didn't tell Jana that part of the time she had been thinking about Jon, too.

"I'm sorry," said Jana. "I wish there was some-thing I could do to help."

"I know you do. You're a great friend. All of you are. But I just don't know what more to do."

"Well, The Fabulous Five have got to stick together!" said Jana. Her voice sounded as if she were ready to fight anyone who argued with her. "We're special, and everyone knows it. I think we should go to the game together and show the whole world that nothing has changed. We're still fabulous. Are you game?"

Jana's loyalty made Christie feel good deep down inside. They had been friends for a long time, and Jana, along with the rest of The Fabulous Five, had never let her down.

"It's too bad we don't still have our Fabulous Five T-shirts," Christie said with a laugh. "We'd *really* show them, if we did."

Christie and Jana called Melanie, Katie, and Beth, and they all agreed that they would meet at Jana's house and go to the game together. Since they didn't have T-shirts, and since Melanie and Beth had to wear their cheerleading outfits, they all agreed to wear two red ribbons in their hair as a symbol of their friendship.

Christie followed Katie and Jana into a row in the cheering section. The stadium was crowded, and it seemed as if everyone from Wacko Junior High was in the stands to watch the Wakeman Warriors play the Milford Mariners.

Christie spotted Melanie and Beth down on the field with the other cheerleaders. Laura McCall and Tammy Lucero were on the field with them and so was Taffy Sinclair.

The crisp fall air felt good, and Christie was glad Jana had talked her into coming. For the first time since yesterday she felt as if everything would work out. Maybe, someday, she would even be able to laugh at her problems.

Just then Tim came walking up the stairs with Kyle Zimmerman, his long legs taking the steps two at a time. He saw Christie and waved. She smiled and waved back. For a second it looked as if he were going to come over to her, but several boys started yelling for him to sit down. Tim yelled back and went to argue with them. Christie wished he had come to talk to her.

She looked around the stands to see who else was there, and she waved at Sara Sawyer and Shawnie

Pendergast. In the row in front of them were Mona Vaughn and Matt Zeboski.

Christie looked to her left. Two rows over, she saw Jon. He was sitting with Kimm Taylor and he had his arm around her. Christie's stomach turned a flip-flop. What was he doing with Kimm? *It's okay*, she told herself, quickly. Calm down. He can do whatever he wants. *I'm the one* who said we should just be friends. But a little voice in the back of her mind asked her, how could Jon date someone else so soon?

CHAPTER

12

*C*hristie tried not to watch Jon and Kimm, but they looked so natural together as they talked and laughed while Jon pointed out things that were happening on the football field. It reminded Christie of how she and Jon had been when they first started dating. They had laughed a lot and played tennis and gone to football games. Being best friends would probably mean they wouldn't do all of those things together anymore. Especially if Jon was dating Kimm. Christie sighed. She knew that being best friends meant not being jealous or making unreasonable demands. Jon was living up to his part of the friendship. Why couldn't she?

After the game, the crowd moved slowly out of the stadium gates. Wacko had won and now had a perfect record of four and oh, and the kids were shouting and holding one finger in the air to show they were number one in the conference.

When Christie and the others reached the field, Beth and Melanie came running up. They shook their pom-pons as they jumped up and down with excitement.

"Wasn't that *fantastic*?" cried Beth. "Did you see Keith's touchdown?"

"It *was* great!" Christie agreed.

"We're NUMBER ONE!" shouted Melanie.

"Let's go to Bumpers and celebrate!" yelled Jana.

Bumpers was packed with Warrior fans who were busy celebrating their team's victory. Clarence Marshall had a big Styrofoam hand with one finger pointing up that he kept shaking in the air as he and Joel Murphy yelled, "NUMBER ONE! NUMBER ONE!"

Christie saw Jon and Kimm come in together. They were holding hands and laughing. Kimm's long black hair swung gracefully to her waist, and her round face and almond eyes were turned up to Jon. She is pretty, Christie thought. And she must be an awfully nice person for Jon to like her.

When Randy Kirwan, Shane Arrington, Keith

Masterson, and the other players came in, everyone started applauding and cheering all over again. The players bowed dramatically to the crowd and then raised both fists as a chant went up. "Wakeman! Wakeman! Wakeman!"

Christie chuckled as she noticed Mr. Matson, who owned Bumpers, covering his ears with both hands. She was pointing him out to the others when Dekeisha Adams and Mandy McDermott came bouncing over to their table.

"What a game! What a game!" Dekeisha shouted. She and Mandy did cheer kicks and nearly knocked Bill Soliday over.

Then Dekeisha's face grew serious. "Did you and Jon break up?" she asked Christie. "I couldn't believe my eyes when I looked up in the stands and saw him with Kimm Taylor."

"We decided that we would be best friends instead of going steady," Christie answered. "He can date whomever he wants." She tried to sound natural.

"Best friends?" Dekeisha looked disbelieving. "You've got to be kidding."

"It's true."

Dekeisha shrugged. "If you say so." Christie could see the doubt in her eyes.

The rest of the afternoon was the pits for Christie. It seemed as if every girl she knew stopped to make some comment about Kimm and Jon—even girls who were supposed to know that they had decided to be just friends. It was as if it were just too much for anyone to believe and so they had to keep checking with her to make sure it was true. She was glad when the afternoon was finally over, and she and her friends were walking home.

"What a day!" Melanie said, laughing. "I think junior high is definitely more fun than elementary school."

"No comparison," said Jana. "Do you remember how the biggest thing that happened to us in the fall was the Halloween party?"

Everyone nodded.

"Remember how Miss Wiggins, our homeroom teacher, used to act so tough?" asked Beth.

"Yes. And then I think she cried when we graduated," said Katie.

"I think she really liked all of us," said Christie. Thinking about Miss Wiggins and Mark Twain Elementary brought back a flood of memories to Christie. They were a lot like the video Jon had made of Wacko, except the pictures didn't flip over. Jana, Katie, Melanie, and Beth were suddenly silent, too.

Christie wondered if they were thinking about their elementary school days, too, and even Miss Wiggins.

Katie broke the silence. "What's everyone going to do tonight?"

"Keith and I are going out," volunteered Beth.

"Randy and I are going bowling with Mom and Pink," said Jana.

"Tony's going to pick up a video, and he, Mom, and I are going to watch it and make popcorn," added Katie.

"Your mom's going to watch with you?" asked Jana incredulously.

"She goes to bed early," Katie assured them. The others laughed.

"Well, I've got a date with Shane," said Melanie. "He asked me at Bumpers."

"Is Igor going with you?" Beth asked, and giggled.

"I asked Shane about that. He said no. Igor peeks too much." Melanie's remarks sent them all into fits of laughter again.

"What are you going to do, Christie?" asked Jana.

"Not much. I'll probably just stay home and watch TV."

"Jon hasn't asked you out?" Everyone waited to hear Christie's answer to Melanie's question.

"I told you we're just friends now. No one seems to be able to believe me."

"It doesn't bother you that he was with Kimm?" asked Katie.

"He can be with whomever he wants," answered Christie stubbornly.

That evening, Christie was glad to be home alone. Her mother and father had gone out, and she popped a gigantic bowl of popcorn and turned on a horror movie. Although the day had started out being fun, she was sick and tired of all the questions about Jon and her. Especially since she had so many questions of her own. Could she really keep from being jealous of Kimm and make a go of this "best friends" business? As much as she wanted it that way, it was certainly harder than she had expected. Still, she *did* need space, and she truly wanted Jon as her friend.

She sank back against the pillows on the couch and stared at the television set without really seeing the movie. She was exhausted and wasn't looking forward to next week. There would probably be more questions about Jon and her, and Melissa was going to talk to Mr. Neal about deciding earlier whether Christie was going to be on the team.

Christie thought about looking up Mr. Neal's telephone number and calling him to tell him she

didn't want to be on the team, anyway. She had totally run out of ideas about how she had gotten the
folder, and she wasn't likely to get any brainstorms
between now and Wednesday. Or Monday, if Melissa
had her way. Calling and quitting might be less em-
barrassing than having Mr. Neal suspend her for
cheating. Besides, she was just plain tired of all of it.

A tear rolled down Christie's cheek. It's not fair,
she thought. I didn't do anything wrong. I work so
hard to get good grades and do what everyone ex-
pects, and now I'm going to be kicked off the team.

Well, she thought, sitting up abruptly and grit-
ting her teeth. That's *exactly* what they're going to
have to do if they want to get rid of me. I can't give
in and let them win when they're the ones who are
wrong. She set her jaw in stubborn determination
and thought, they're going to have to kick me off
because I'm not quitting!

CHAPTER

13

Christie dreaded walking onto the school grounds on Monday morning. She felt as if everyone were watching her as she marched to her execution. This must be the way Joan of Arc felt on the way to be burned at the stake, she thought.

Jana, Melanie, Beth, and Katie were waiting at The Fabulous Five's favorite spot by the fence.

After they had all said hi to her, Katie nodded toward the spot where The Fantastic Foursome usually met in the morning. "Do you see anything different about them?"

"Melissa's not with them?" Christie asked.

"That's right," said Jana. "She went into the building right after we got here."

"And she looked at us and smiled before she went in," added Beth.

Christie's flesh crawled. "She obviously went in to talk to Mr. Neal."

"That's what we thought," agreed Katie. Gloom settled over The Fabulous Five as they waited for the first bell to ring.

Suddenly the school doors popped open, and Melissa came flying out of the building with a big smile on her face.

"I don't think there's much doubt about what happened," said Katie.

"I don't either," said Christie, trying to sound cheerful. "Well, I didn't do anything wrong, and I'm not going to act as if I did. If Mr. Neal is going to suspend me from the team, that's just the way it's going to be."

"Thataway, Christie," said Katie. "I just wish we could get whoever put that folder with your books in front of the Teen Court. I'd vote for hanging them."

The rest of the morning was terrible for Christie. Even though she had made up her mind that she had done nothing wrong and shouldn't feel bad about whatever happened, it was like waiting for the other shoe to drop. Only it's more like the next cannon to shoot, thought Christie, because I'm going to be dead anyway.

In her last class before noon, Christie's teacher gave her an envelope. Christie stayed after everyone else had left with the envelope lying in the center of her desk. She wondered if prison wardens delivered the death sentence to convicts on death row in an envelope like this one.

She chewed her lower lip as she tore it open.

> *Christie Winchell:*
> *Please see me in my office after lunch.*
> *Mr. Neal*

I might have those words put on my tombstone when I die, Christie thought.

"I'm sorry, Christie," Mr. Neal said, after he told her of his decision. He did look sorry, she thought, but not nearly as sorry as I am.

As Mr. Neal had explained it, Melissa had convinced him that it wouldn't be fair for him to wait until Wednesday to decide who would be on the Super Quiz team. Since there weren't any clues that would prove Christie hadn't taken the folder she was off the team.

"If we had *anything* that would show you accidentally got the questions, Christie, I could do something," Mr. Neal repeated. "But the way it is now, I have no choice."

Christie's stomach turned over. She thought she was going to be sick.

"Come to me if you find out something." Mr. Neal continued. "I'm going to have the team together in the media center after school for a practice. I'll have to tell them about the change then."

Christie left the office and plodded down the hall like a zombie. For a second she considered faking being sick so she could go home, but then she decided not to. That would just make Melissa McConnell, Laura McCall, and the others feel as if they had really beaten her. She couldn't give them that satisfaction, no matter what.

Christie put her money in the vending machine and pulled the lever. A bag of chips dropped into the trough. She couldn't face going into the cafeteria at noon where she would be stared at, so she walked outside and found a quiet place to sit.

She was off the Super Quiz team. She said it over and over to herself, trying to get used to the idea now that it was definite. How was she going to tell her parents? They were *so* proud of her. Her mother even thought she was smarter than her brothers, one of whom was an attorney and the other in medical school. How was she going to tell them? Christie gulped hard and stuck her chin out. And Friday after school everyone would be at the Super Quiz match between Wakeman and Trumbull. Tears built up behind her eyes, but she refused to let them out.

"Hey, Christie!" Jon's voice broke through the gloom that filled her mind. "I've been looking all over for you. Where have you been? I thought for sure I'd see you in the cafeteria."

Christie smiled at him weakly and started to explain.

"Never mind," Jon interrupted. "You won't believe what I've got! You just won't believe it."

Christie looked at his beaming face. He was smiling from ear to ear and his brown eyes were gleaming as she had never seen them gleam before.

"Do you know what this is?" he asked as he held up a small black box.

CHAPTER

14

"Of course I know what that is," Christie answered Jon. "It's a videotape. So what?"

"It's not just any old videotape," Jon said proudly.

"It's one I made last Thursday when The Dreadful Alternatives were setting up on stage. Remember? Mr. Neal was doing the walk-through with the Super Quiz team."

"Oh, yeah," Christie mumbled. She was glad that Jon felt excited about the tape, but right now she just wanted to be alone.

"Come on," said Jon, grabbing her hand and

pulling her. "I've got to show you this." Christie went along reluctantly to the media center.

Mrs. Karl said Jon could use a VCR, and he quickly started setting up the tape as Christie slid into a chair.

"Okay, hold on to your seat," he said with a smile. "You're about to see the greatest show on earth."

The video started with shots of the band from different parts of the stage. "I was testing to see where I could get the best pictures," said Jon. "I wanted to find the best places to shoot from. You know, for lighting and stuff. Of course the spotlights will be on during a regular performance, but this will give me an idea where to set up. As you can see, I had to shoot through a lot of other people to get the band."

It was true. On the tape the kids from the Super Quiz team were walking all over the stage, totally oblivious as they passed in front of his camera. There were pictures of Mr. Neal at the podium with the band in the background, and at one point the custodian pushing the broom walked directly at the camera's lens.

Why is he showing me this? thought Christie. There's nothing interesting about this video. It's just a bunch of people milling around. But Jon was staring intently at the television.

"Now! Here it comes," he said, grabbing her hand.

Christie stared at the TV. Kimm was talking to one of the guys with a guitar, and the drummer was working on setting up his drums. She could see Tim Riggs and Brad Cochran watching Mr. Neal at the podium.

"There! Behind Mr. Neal. Watch the custodian!" said Jon excitedly. The custodian was wiping off one of the long tables that the Super Quiz team would use the next morning.

Christie leaned closer to watch as the custodian moved some books around to clean. Then he picked up a blue folder and put it on top of another stack of books. *That's Mr. Neal's blue folder and those are MY books he put it on!* Christie's eyes opened wide in amazement. Next the custodian moved part of Christie's books and then put the rest on top. Christie stared in fascination as Mr. Neal's blue folder ended up in the middle of her books.

"Did you see it?" asked Jon. "Just like shuffling cards." A grin spread from one of his ears to the other.

Christie bounced up and down in her seat and

clapped her hands. "Play it again! Play it again!" Jon ran the tape back slightly and hit play.

There it was, right before her eyes. The custodian moving the books around so that Mr. Neal's blue folder was in between two of her books.

"I must have brought the folder home in my stack of books on Thursday night and not noticed it until the tryouts Friday morning, when I thought my mom had put it there," she said in amazement. She grabbed Jon around the neck and hugged him hard.

"I love it! I love it!" she squealed, and kissed him.

"HUMPH!" Mrs. Karl was looking at them from her desk.

Christie's face turned hot and she knew she was as red as a beet, but she didn't care. She had proof now that she *hadn't* taken Mr. Neal's folder. Everyone would know that she hadn't cheated. She looked at Jon appreciatively and then took his hand and squeezed it.

He smiled back, and his brown eyes sparkled. "What are best friends for?" he asked softly.

CHAPTER

15

"Quiet, please, everyone," Mr. Neal said loudly. "It's time for roll call.

"Daphne?"

"Here."

"Brad?"

"Here."

Mr. Neal continued calling the names, and when he called out Christie's, several heads turned toward her. Melissa McConnell looked first shocked and then angry.

When Mr. Neal finished, he closed his notebook and placed it on top of the infamous blue folder. "Before we get started, I'm going to turn the floor over to Christie for a few moments. She has something very interesting to show you." He smiled and took a seat in the front row.

Without saying anything, Christie got up and marched to the front of the media center where the television stood on a tall stand that made it easy to see. She turned it on, punched the play button on the VCR, and stepped aside.

The same images flashed on the screen as she had seen when Jon first showed her the tape. The band was setting up. Kids from the Super Quiz team were milling around. Then Jon stepped forward and speeded up the tape. The custodian came charging across the room with his broom and Mr. Neal moved in herky-jerky motions that made all the kids laugh. Christie looked at Mr. Neal, and even he was smiling at the way he looked.

As the videotape reached the point where the custodian was cleaning the table, Jon slowed it again, and when the custodian put the blue folder on her books, it stopped. Christie looked at the faces of the Super Quiz team, and their eyes were fixed on the television screen.

Then the custodian started cleaning again, and when he moved half of her books, the video stopped so no one could miss what was happening. The frame froze once more when he placed the books on top of the blue folder, sandwiching it in between. The room was deathly quiet as everyone stared transfixed at the television set.

"*That's how* Mr. Neal's folder got in with my books," said Christie loudly so everyone could hear.

The kids in the room started applauding and Tim began shouting and punching his fist into the air. No one paid any attention to the rest of the video.

Shivers of joy ran through Christie, and the tears she had held back so long ran down her cheeks as she stood in front of the Super Quiz team and listened to their cheers. She smiled at Jon, who stood in the back. He returned her smile, gave her a thumbs-up, and walked out of the room.

"Wait!" Christie cried as she raced after him. He was more important than all the Super Quiz teams in the world, and she had to tell him so.

"Jon?" she called shyly when she reached the hallway and saw that he had stopped to wait for her. "Can I talk to you a minute?"

"Sure," he said.

"I just want you to know that you're the best friend anyone could ever have. No matter what happens, I'll never forget this."

Jon chuckled softly. "Want to know a secret?"

Christie nodded.

"I'm not the one who spotted the blue folder in the tape. In fact, I was so busy thinking about all the technical stuff that I wasn't really paying much attention to what anyone in the film was doing."

Christie frowned. "What do you mean?" she sputtered. "Of course you did. Otherwise . . ." She shook her head and raised both arms in a helpless shrug. "Otherwise how . . ."

Jon held up his hand. "Kimm was the one who noticed it. Like everybody else in school, she had heard about the mess you were in over the folder and the questions, and when she looked at the tape, it was the first thing she saw."

"Kimm?" Christie whispered in astonishment.

"That's right," said Jon. "I tried to get her to come along and take the credit, but she wouldn't. She even made me promise that I wouldn't tell you. She knows that things have been a little rocky between us lately, and she not only wanted to make sure you got out of trouble, but that you and I patched things up with each other."

Christie swallowed hard. "She sounds terrific to do a thing like that."

Jon nodded. "I have a feeling the two of you are going to be friends, too."

Christie smiled to herself as she watched him walk away a few minutes later. Their special friendship would probably last forever, and now she knew there was no way that she would ever be jealous of Kimm again either. Kimm was a special person, just as Jon was, and everything was truly going to be all right from now on.

The score was tied at one hundred eighty each, and the moderator was taking a few minutes to confer with the judges. It was the third and last match between the Wakeman and Trumbull Super Quiz teams, and they had each won one game. Christie could feel the tension among the players, and the audience was getting noisier and noisier as the match drew near its end.

She could see The Fabulous Five sitting five rows back. Beth had her head in her hands and was rocking back and forth dramatically in her excitement. Melanie had her eyes covered, as if she were afraid to look, and Jana and Katie were sitting on the edges of their seats.

Christie's mother and father sat farther back. She smiled at them and wondered if they could see her face.

Curtis fidgeted at Christie's left, and Tim frowned and stared hard at the blank paper in front of him on her right. The three of them, along with Daphne, Kyle, and Pam, had started out by losing the first game, and they had trailed in the second before surging ahead by answering the last five questions. The last game had been a neck-and-neck battle all the way.

Christie looked across the stage at the table where the Trumbull team sat. They're good, she thought. If we beat them, we'll be very lucky.

Rodney Cox slouched back in his chair, frowning and running his fingers through his red hair. He had looked arrogant during the first game and the first half of the second, when Trumbull was beating Wakeman, but the cocky look had disappeared when Wakeman pulled even and then won the second game. He looked like a volcano about to erupt when Kyle took a question on the rebound from one of Rodney's teammates to tie the score at one eighty. Christie didn't think she would like Rodney very much.

"All right, everyone," Mr. Perdyne, the moderator, said. "Here is the final question. And, may I say, both teams have fought gallantly. Good luck to you both on this one." He pulled an index card from the box in front of him.

"The category is social studies," he said, and then paused.

Rats. Social studies, thought Christie. I wish it were math or current events. She had done well in those categories and had helped the Wakeman team to win the second game.

"Who," Mr. Perdyne continued, "was the person who fought for women's right to vote, and was eventually honored by having her likeness placed on a silver dollar?"

Christie's hand streaked to the button in front of her. At the same time she saw a flash of movement across the room at Rodney Cox's position. A buzzer sounded and she looked up to see the Wakeman light was lit. She had beaten him. Thank you, Katie Shannon, she thought.

The whole Trumbull team was leaning forward staring at Christie, and she could feel her teammates' eyes on her.

"Go get'em, Christie," she heard Tim say in a low voice.

"The person who fought for women's right to vote and had her likeness put on a silver dollar was Susan B. Anthony," Christie said as loudly and clearly as she could.

"The answer is correct," said the moderator. "*The match goes to Wakeman Junior High.*"

Cheers burst from the audience and Christie saw The Fabulous Five jumping up and down. Curtis slapped her on the back so hard it hurt, and Brad shook both fists.

Christie smiled so broadly she thought her face might crack. She could see her mother and father standing and applauding. They were probably telling everyone near them that she was their daughter, she mused. At the side of the auditorium she saw Jon with his camcorder trained on her, and she clasped her hands above her head victoriously the way prize fighters do and mugged for the camera.

Behind her, she heard Tim call her name. She turned to thank him for his encouragement, but before she could get the words out, he scooped her up into a gigantic hug. She stiffened for an instant, remembering Jon, and then she relaxed and hugged Tim back.

CHAPTER

16

"Well, what do you think?" asked Christie. "Should we order the red T-shirts or the gold ones?"

The Fabulous Five were sitting in Christie's family room. Two delivery boxes were on the coffee table with the remains of one sausage pizza and one deep-dish pepperoni, mushroom, and green-pepper pizza, which was Jana's favorite. T-shirt catalogs were spread out all over the floor, and the girls were lying around looking at them.

"I vote for red!" yelled Beth, talking around a string of cheese that she had stretched out from her mouth to as far as she could reach. "With THE FABULOUS FIVE in gold letters."

"I vote for gold!" yelled Katie. "With red lettering. The red shirt would look terrible with my red hair."

"It would not," said Beth, letting the cheese dangle back into her mouth.

"Look," said Melanie, holding a catalog up to Katie's face and placing a lock of her hair over the sample color. "It goes perfectly with your hair color."

"I think so, too," said Beth.

"And red and gold are Wacko Junior High's colors," said Jana. "All of the Wacko teams wear red tops, so it just makes sense, if we're going to use the school colors, that we have red with gold lettering."

"I really think it will look good on you, Katie," said Christie.

"Oh, all right, but are we going to put our names on them, too?"

"I think it would be a good idea," agreed Jana, reaching for another slice of pizza. "We could put them in different positions, like when we write things on our notebooks."

"Great idea!" said Beth. "Boy, will Laura and the rest of The Fantastic Foursome be green with envy."

"I bet they get T-shirts when they see ours," said Melanie.

"But they won't be able to use the school colors, and everyone will know they're copying us," said Christie.

"Yea, for The Fabulous Five!" yelled Beth. "First again!"

"YEA!" they all yelled, holding slices of pizza in the air.

"Changing the subject," said Jana, "I'm sure glad things turned out all right for you with the Super Quiz team, Christie."

"*You're* glad?" said Christie, rolling her eyes. "I thought I was dead. If we hadn't been able to prove how Mr. Neal's questions got with my books, I wouldn't be able to hold my head up in school or at home. Jon and Kimm saved me with his video recording."

"And now you're the hero of Wacko Junior High," said Jana. "It's super the way it worked out."

"What I think is a riot, is the way the last question turned out to be the one that Katie kept asking you," Melanie added. "I guess Katie's being a feminist paid off for you this time, Christie."

Christie looked at Katie and smiled. "It sure did. Katie, I'll never, ever, get on you again about being too much of a liberated woman."

"I don't think she's as liberated as she wants us to believe," said Beth. "Look at the Macho guy she dates."

"You just don't understand Tony," Katie responded. "He's really a kind and sensitive person."

"Now you sound like Jana when she talks about Randy," interjected Melanie. "By the way, how's your nonromance going with Jon, Christie?"

"Fine. He has a date with Kimm for Saturday."

"That's probably the last you'll see of him," said Melanie.

"No. Not true. We're going to play tennis Saturday morning, and he'll be over a couple of nights a week to study. Besides, I'm really starting to like Kimm. I'm sure everything's going to work out fine."

"Now you can look at the other boys again," said Melanie. "There are a lot of yummy ones. But stay away from Scott, Shane, and Garrett. They're mine."

"Sheez!" said Katie. "You'd think every boy in Wacko was her personal property."

"No, I don't," Melanie said with a pouty look on her face. "I'd never go after guys that any of you four were dating."

"Just kidding," responded Katie.

"No. I really don't want to date right away," said Christie. "I broke up with Jon because I wanted more space, and getting another boyfriend right away might put me right back where I was. And it might make Jon think I wanted to break up just so I could date someone else, and that's not true. I'll date eventually, but not right now."

"I saw Jon's video of The Dreadful Alternatives in Mr. Levine's acting class the other day," said Beth. "He showed it to us as a good example of what can be done with a home video camera."

"What's Jon going to do with his movies? Anything?" asked Katie.

"I think he might," said Christie. "He was telling me that his mother and father like what he's doing, and his mother asked him if she could include part of this last one as a clip in one of her news shows. It would be a little thing about The Dreadful Alternatives.

"I think he might just be starting to feel pretty good about himself. Who knows? He might even end up with a career in screen photography."

After the others had left, Christie cleaned up in the family room and threw away the empty pizza boxes. She stuck her head in the living room and said good-night to her mother and father and went up to her room.

She hummed to herself as she brushed her hair and smiled. The face of a happy, blond-haired girl smiled back at her from the mirror.

Everything had turned out so great. A week ago

she was in the pits, and now she was the school hero-
ine for answering the question that won the match
for Wakeman. Of course Kyle, Pam, Tim, Daphne,
and Curtis had gotten a lot of answers right, too. It
just happened that she got the last question.

She could still hear Tim's voice telling her to "Go
get'em, Christie!" He was nice. And a good hugger,
she thought with a giggle. But she didn't want to
jump in and start dating right away. The last thing
she needed was another commitment. She'd just
wait to see who was available that she might like to
go out with. When the right person came along and
asked her, she'd start dating again.

CHAPTER

17

*B*eth was panting when she caught up with Jana, Katie, Christie, and Melanie on the way to Bumpers. "*I did it! I did it!*" she squealed, jumping up and down.

"What did you do?" asked Christie as they all bent to help pick up the books she had dropped in her excitement.

"The play! Mr. Levine told me I get to try out for the *lead role* in the play." She whirled around, billowing her long skirt and looking as if she were a ballerina.

"And Mr. Levine said his friend, Mr. Stapleton,

who's a casting director from New York, will be here to help with the casting. Maybe he'll like me. This will be the biggest part I've ever tried out for in my *whole* life. *This may be the start to my acting career.*"

"All *right*!" shouted Melanie.

"Oh, I'm so glad," said Jana. "It's a great chance for you." They crowded around Beth and hugged her, laughing and chattering happily.

As they continued walking toward Bumpers, Katie looked at Beth and asked cautiously, "Uh, who else is trying out?"

"Mr. Levine said Kaci Davis, Laura McCall, and Taffy Sinclair have signed up, too."

Katie let out a low whistle. "That's pretty tough competition."

"It sure is," said Melanie.

"I can do it, though. I know I can," Beth responded, sticking out her chin. "I want it *so* badly, all I have to do is try my hardest."

"We know you can," said Jana. "Is there anything we can do to help?"

"Not really. I just have to learn my part and practice like mad. And if I win, we'll have practice three nights a week until opening night."

"And then you'll have homework the other nights," said Christie, "and cheerleading practice after school. I guess we won't be seeing much of you for a while. Have you talked to Keith? How does he feel about losing you for such a long time?"

"Keith and I have been going together since the sixth grade. I know he'll understand. He won't care," she said confidently, but she couldn't help remembering the odd look on his face when she had told him about the play and how much time the practices would take.

"I don't know about that," said Melanie. "I wouldn't want to take a chance on being out of circulation like that for that long. I'm not sure Scott would understand."

"I *won't* be out of circulation," protested Beth. "I'll see him at school, and Bumpers, and we can still date some."

"You remember what happened to me when I tried to do too much," responded Melanie. "*Mono, the kissing disease*," she said, making a monster face and holding her hands up as if they were claws.

"Won't your parents keep you from going out as much as you have?" asked Jana. "They know what happened to Melanie."

"My mother would ground me if I were out every night during the week," added Katie.

"Oh, you guys are just worrywarts," said Beth. "Everything will be great between Keith and me."

But she couldn't forget that look on Keith's face, and a little spot of doubt formed deep inside of her mind and started to grow.

Will everything be okay between Beth and Keith, or will Beth have to make a choice between stardom and romance? Find out in the *The Fabulous Five #10: PLAYING THE PART.*

ABOUT THE AUTHOR

Betsy Haynes, the daughter of a former news-woman, began scribbling poetry and short stories as soon as she learned to write. A serious writing career, however, had to wait until after her marriage and the arrival of her two children. But that early practice must have paid off, for within three months Mrs. Haynes had sold her first story. In addition to a number of magazine short stories and the Taffy Sinclair series, Mrs. Haynes is also the author of *The Great Mom Swap* and its sequel, *The Great Boyfriend Trap.* She lives in Colleyville, Texas, with her husband, who is also an author.

IT'S THE FABULOUS FIVE!

From Betsy Haynes, the bestselling author of the Taffy Sinclair books, *The Great Mom Swap*, and *The Great Boyfriend Trap*, comes THE FABULOUS FIVE. Follow the adventures of Jana Morgan and the rest of THE FABULOUS FIVE as they begin the new school year in Wakeman Jr. High.

☐ **SEVENTH-GRADE RUMORS (Book #1)** 15625-X $2.75

☐ **THE TROUBLE WITH FLIRTING (Book #2)** 15633-0 $2.75

☐ **THE POPULARITY TRAP (Book #3)** 15634-9 $2.75

☐ **HER HONOR, KATIE SHANNON (Book #4)** 15640-3 $2.75

☐ **THE BRAGGING WAR (Book #5)** 15651-9 $2.75

☐ **THE PARENT GAME (Book #6)** 15670-5 $2.75

☐ **THE KISSING DISASTER (Book #7)** 15710-8 $2.75

☐ **THE RUNAWAY CRISIS (Book #8)** 15719-1 $2.75

☐ **THE BOYFRIEND DILEMMA (Book #9)** 15720-5 $2.75

Buy them at your local bookstore or use this page to order:

- -

Bantam Books, Dept. SK28, 414 East Golf Road, Des Plaines, IL 60016

Please send me the books I have checked above. I am enclosing $_____ (please add $2.00 to cover postage and handling). Send check or money order—no cash or C.O.D.s please.

Mr/Ms _____

Address _____

City/State _____ Zip _____

SK28—6/89

Please allow four to six weeks for delivery. This offer expires 12/89.

Great FREE offer just for you!

Join SNEAK PEEKS™!

Do you want to know what's new before anyone else? Do you like to read great books about girls just like you? If you do, then you won't want to miss SNEAK PEEKS™! Be the first of your friends to know what's hot ... When you join SNEAK PEEKS™, we'll send you FREE inside information in the mail about the latest books ... *before they're published!* Plus updates on your favorite series, authors, and exciting new stories filled with friendship and fun ... adventure and mystery ... girlfriends and boyfriends.

It's easy to be a member of SNEAK PEEKS™. Just fill out the coupon below ... and get ready for fun! It's FREE! Don't delay—sign up today!

Saddle up for great reading with

THE SADDLE CLUB

A blue-ribbon series by Bonnie Bryant

Stevie, Carole and Lisa are all very different, but they *love* horses! The three girls are best friends at Pine Hollow Stables, where they ride and care for all kinds of horses. Come to Pine Hollow and get ready for all the fun and adventure that comes with being 13!

Don't miss this terrific ten-book series. Collect them all!

☐ 15594 **HORSE CRAZY #1** $2.75
☐ 15611 **HORSE SHY #2** $2.75
☐ 15626 **HORSE SENSE #3** $2.75
☐ 15637 **HORSE POWER #4** $2.75
☐ 15703 **TRAIL MATES #5** $2.75

Watch for other SADDLE CLUB books all year. More great reading—and riding—to come!